For all the brilliant teachers who are missed when they're out sick
(especially our sisters), and all the generous substitutes
who make it okay in the end
—A.V. & L.G.S.

For Lydie
—C.R.

Text copyright © 2018 by Liz Garton Scanlon and Audrey Vernick
Illustrations copyright © 2018 by Chris Raschka

First Edition, June 2018
10 9 8 7 6 5 4 3 2 1
FAC-019191-18138
Printed in Malaysia

This book is set in Cala Light/Fontspring
Designed by Phil Caminiti
Illustrations created with watercolor and gouache on paper

Library of Congress Cataloging-in-Publication Data

Names: Scanlon, Elizabeth Garton, author. • Vernick, Audrey, author. •
Raschka, Christopher, illustrator.
Title: Dear substitute / by Liz Garton Scanlon and Audrey Vernick ; illustrated by Chris Raschka.
Description: First edition. • Los Angeles ; New York : Disney/HYPERION, 2018.
Summary: In a series of letters a student laments the absence of her teacher and daily routine, but she soon realizes
there are benefits to mixing things up, and that perhaps having a substitute teacher is not so bad after all.
Identifiers: LCCN 2016054231 • ISBN 9781484750223 (hardcover) • ISBN 1484750225 (hardcover)
Subjects: CYAC: Substitute teachers—Fiction. • Schools—Fiction. •
Letters—Fiction.
Classification: LCC PZ7.S2798 De 2018 • DDC [E]—dc23
LC record available at https://lccn.loc.gov/2016054231

Reinforced binding
Visit www.DisneyBooks.com

Dear Substitute

by Liz Garton Scanlon and Audrey Vernick
pictures by Chris Raschka

Disney • HYPERION

Los Angeles   New York

Dear Substitute,

Wow. This is a surprise.

What are you doing here?

Where's Mrs. Giordano,

and why didn't she warn us?

Dear Attendance,

You're not quite right today.

The substitute doesn't know

how to pronounce anything.

Poor Charvi and Betje.

Poor Eliandrea.

Dear Homework That I Stayed Up Late Doing,

Guess what?

You're not being collected until

Mrs. Giordano gets back.

I could've shot more baskets last night after all.

Dear Pledge,

I pledge allegiance

to Mrs. Giordano.

I like her more today than I normally do.

Dear Library,

The substitute says
we're not coming to you,
even though it's Tuesday,
and I remembered
to bring back my book.

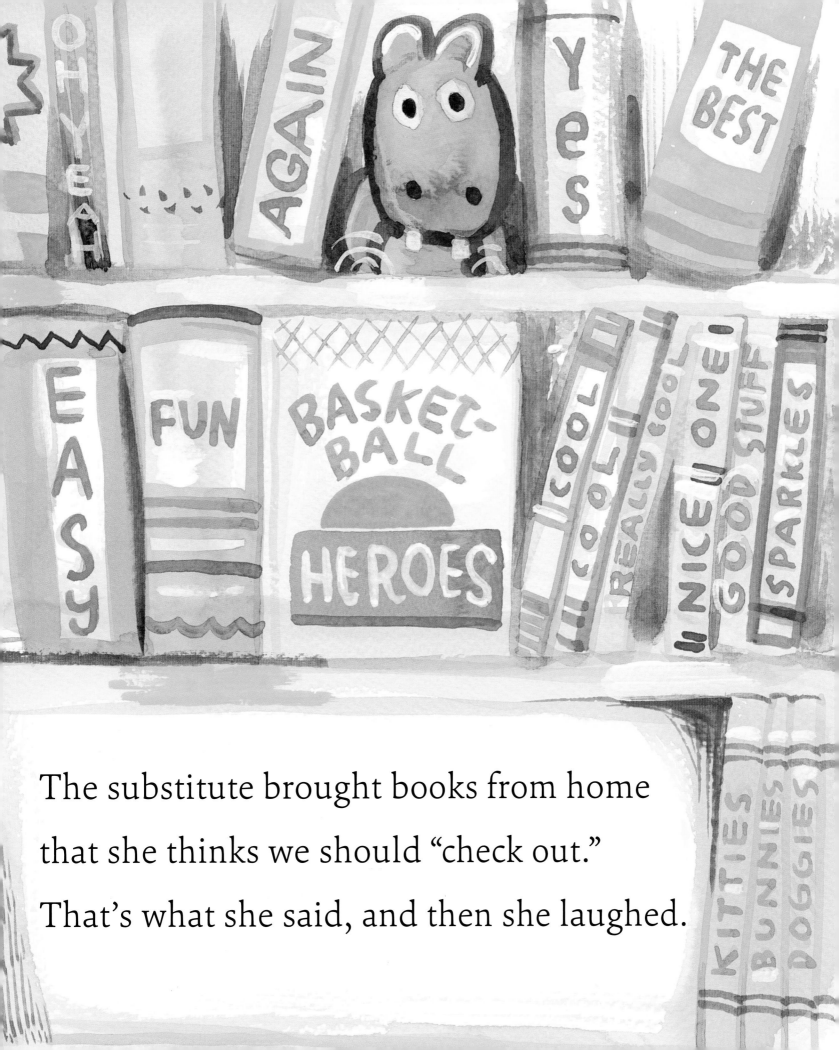

The substitute brought books from home that she thinks we should "check out." That's what she said, and then she laughed.

Dear Turtle,

We're supposed to clean your tank today.

It's Tank Tuesday—everyone knows that!

The substitute says maybe tomorrow.

Please don't explode, or die of dirt, or escape.

PS: Mrs. Giordano would never skip

tank-cleaning day.

Dear Class Rules,

We have you for a reason.

And one of the rules should be:

the whole day can't be

changed around by a sub named Miss Pelly.

"Pelly like a pelican," she told us.

And then she laughed—again.

Miss Pelly doesn't take anything seriously.

S.O.S.

Miss Pelly →

Me →

Dear Line,

Yes, I *do* know I'm supposed

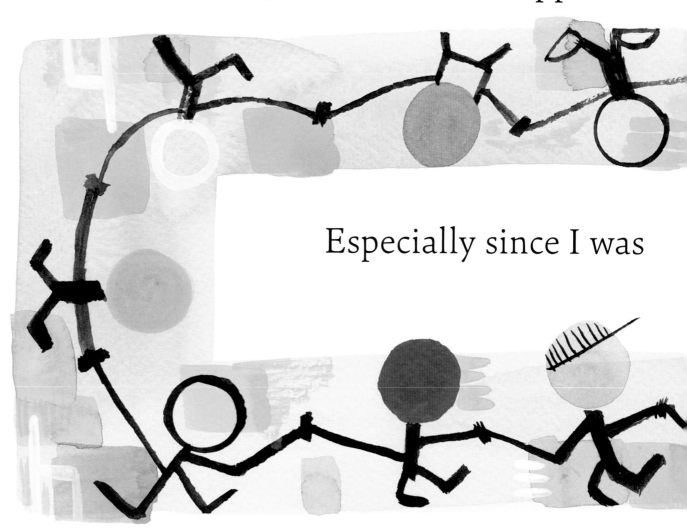

Especially since I was

I'm sorry that You-Know-Who doesn't

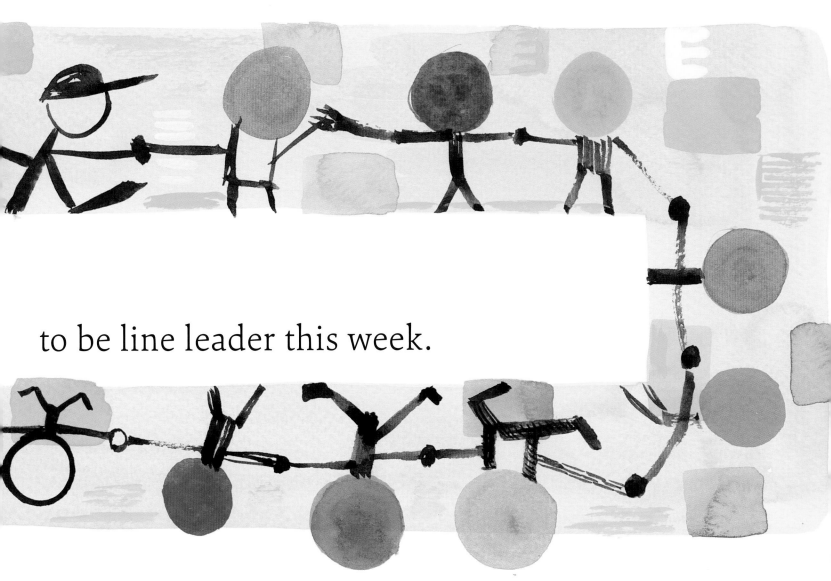

to be line leader this week.

chair stacker last week.

know how we do things in Room 102.

Dear Lunch,

At least in here, everything's the same.

Including chocolate milk and trading food with Connor. (Even though trading food is not exactly allowed.)

Dear Miss Pelly,

Now you care about rules?

How did you even see us swapping?

I think you have what my mom has:

back-of-the-head eyes.

I'm sorry. I wasn't thinking about

people being allergic to things.

I was just thinking about Connor's yummy chips.

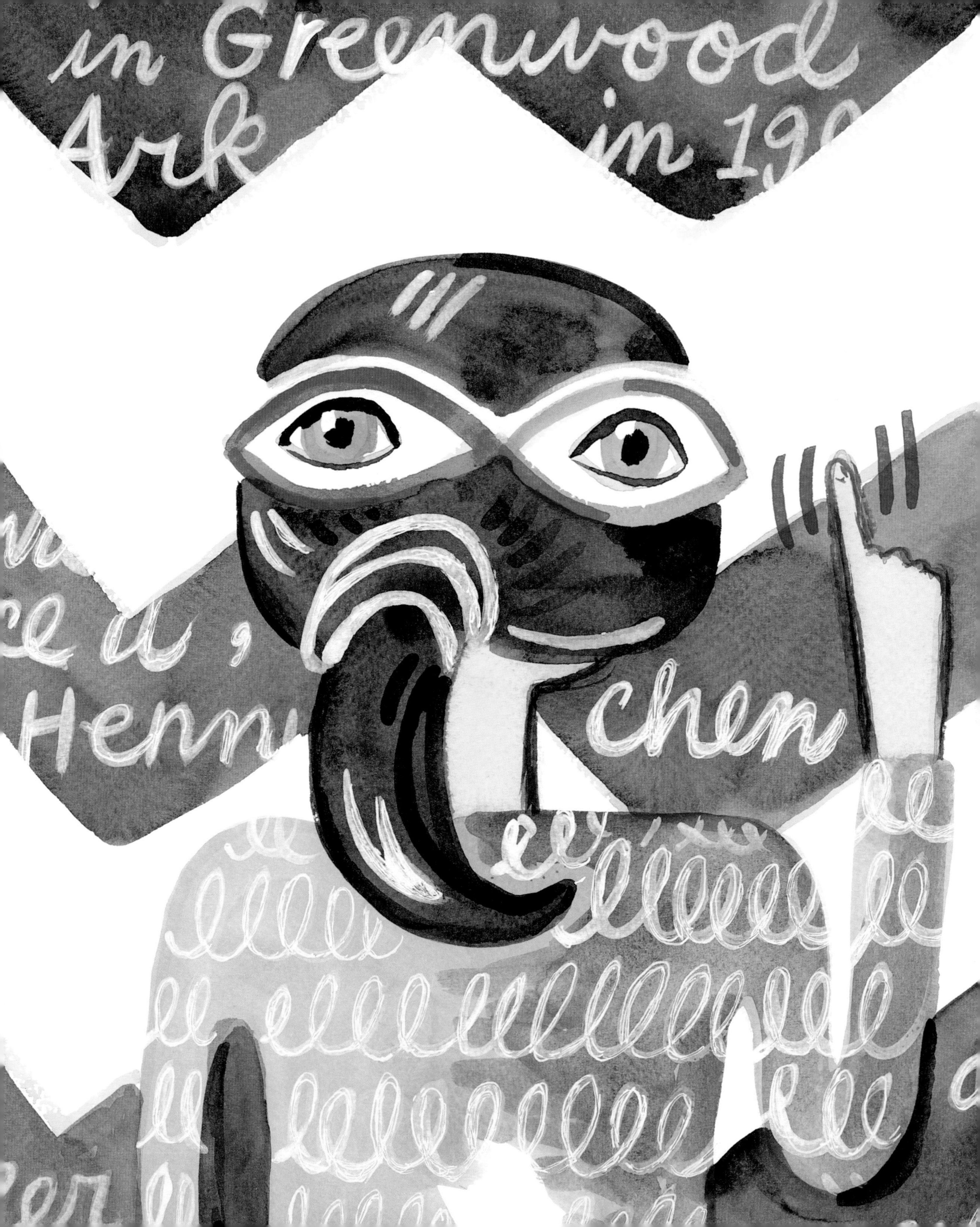
in Greenwood
Ark
in 190
Henn
chen

Dear Tears,

Not here.

Not now.

You understand.

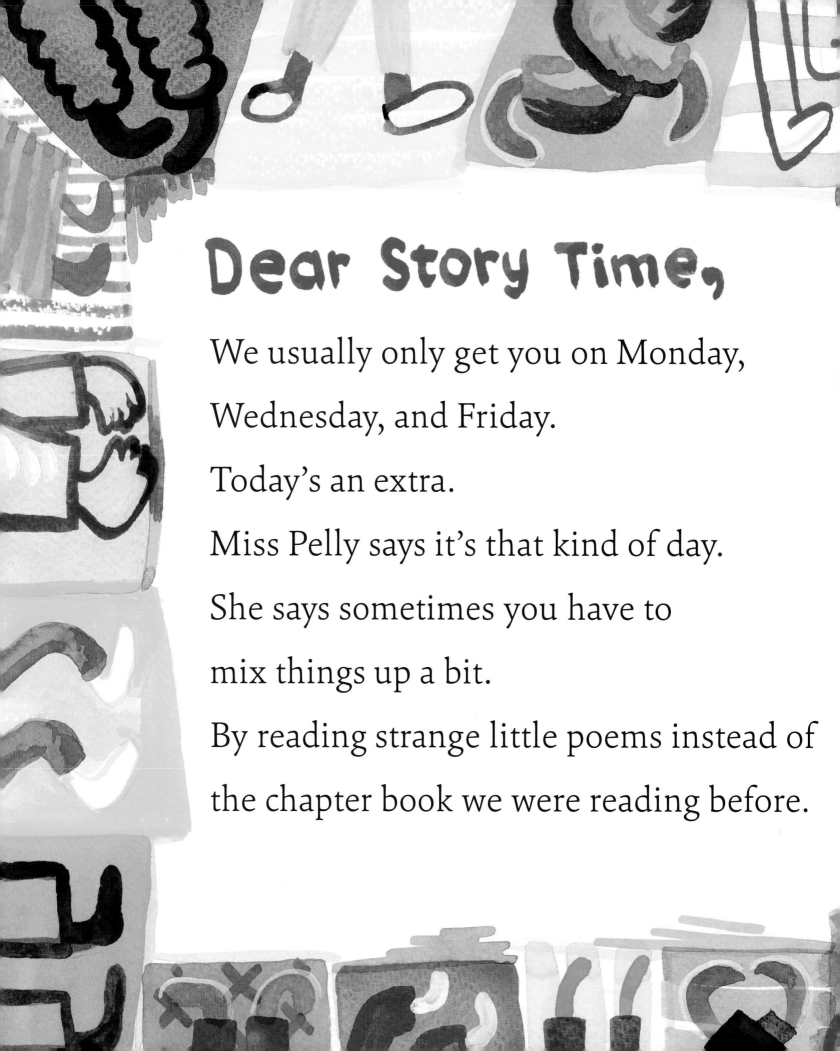

Dear Story Time,

We usually only get you on Monday,

Wednesday, and Friday.

Today's an extra.

Miss Pelly says it's that kind of day.

She says sometimes you have to

mix things up a bit.

By reading strange little poems instead of

the chapter book we were reading before.

Dear World,

It turns out I really like poetry.

Especially funny poetry.

Especially funny poetry about pelicans.

And crocodiles. And underwear.

Dear Turtle,

Here's a poem I made up:

A funny old friend is Turtle

If he doesn't die of the dirt-le.

He's got a tough shell

That helps him not smell.

Tomorrow we'll get water and

squirtle (him)!

PS: Miss Pelly helped.

Dear Miss Pelly,

I wonder what kind of food *you*

bring in *your* lunch?

I might write another poem.

It might be about surprises.

And back-of-the-head eyes-es.

And a switched-around day that's A-OK.

And a substitute who likes kiwi fruit.

PS: Do you?

Dear Mrs. Giordano,

It's okay if you're not quite ready

to come back tomorrow.

We're doing fine.

I mean, not exactly like if you were here.

But sometimes you've got to

mix things up a little.

You know?